LITTLE WOLF AND THE MOON

by Marjorie Dennis Murray
Illustrated by Stacey Schuett

MARSHALL CAVENDISH   NEW YORK

Text copyright © 2002 by Marjorie Dennis Murray
Illustrations copyright © 2002 by Stacey Schuett
All rights reserved.
Marshall Cavendish, 99 White Plains Road, Tarrytown, NY 10591
www.marshallcavendish.com

Library of Congress Cataloging-in-Publication Data
Murray, Marjorie Dennis.
Little Wolf and the moon / by Marjorie Dennis Murray.
p. cm.
Summary: Every night, Little Wolf looks up at the moon and wonders why it is the way it is.
ISBN 0-7614-5100-5
[1. Wolves—Fiction. 2. Moon—Fiction. 3. Animals—Infancy—Fiction.] I. Title.
PZ7.M9635 Li 2002   [E]—dc21   00-052317

The text of this book is set in 17 point Stone Sans.
The illustrations in this book are rendered in watercolor.
Printed in Malaysia

First edition

1 3 5 6 4 2

For my brother Dan, my kindred spirit;
and Catherine Jontos-Putnam, my favorite poet;
and for Fritz, my own Little Wolf.
—M.D.M.

For Lisa, Devin, and Jared
—S.S.

Every night when the earth was dark and silent,
Little Wolf came out of the forest to look at the moon.

The earth was wide, the forest was tall, and
under the moon, Little Wolf felt very small.

How does the moon stay up in the sky? wondered Little Wolf. Why doesn't it fall? For a long time he thought and wondered.

Then the moon slipped behind a cloud and Little Wolf went back to the forest.

One night Little Wolf watched the moon
climb above the stars.
How does the moon climb over the stars?
wondered Little Wolf. Why is the moon so large?

For a long time he thought and wondered.
   The earth was wide, the forest was tall, and under
the moon, Little Wolf felt very small.

Soon Little Wolf's brothers and sisters came with him to look at the moon. They romped and howled under its light, lifting their voices in a wolf song.

Rabbits and mice scattered over the fields,
stirring the night.

Little Wolf stayed long after they had gone.
Beneath the moon he sat alone.

How does the moon shine at night? he wondered.
Where does the moon get its light? For a long time
he thought and wondered.

Then the moon hid behind the clouds and Little
Wolf went back to the forest.

In autumn Little Wolf romped through golden fields.

At night he watched the harvest moon. It loomed heavy in the sky and Little Wolf caught the scent of winter.

The wind blew cold, the forest stretched tall, and under the harvest moon Little Wolf felt very small.

Soon the snow came and the earth glistened
under the moon.

There is nothing so beautiful as the winter moon,
thought Little Wolf. What could be more wondrous
than the moon?

The earth glistened, the trees stretched tall,
and under the winter moon Little Wolf felt very,
very small.

That night, in the forest, Little Wolf nestled close to his brothers and sisters. The snow glistened.

The stars twinkled and he drifted off to sleep.

High above, in the heavens, the moon looked
down on Little Wolf.

The wind stirred, ruffling Little Wolf's silvery fur.

How wondrous, thought the moon. The
moonwolf is dreaming. Some nights he plays
in the forest, some nights he sings in the
meadow, and some nights he dreams.

Why does he play? wondered the moon. Why does he sing? Why does he gaze at the heavens? And why does he dream?

Then a cloud swept over Little Wolf and the moon could no longer see him.

The next night, in the forest, Little Wolf
looked up at the trees that grew so tall. Their
branches spread stark and still against the winter
sky. Beyond the sky, out in the starry heavens,
the moon looked down on Little Wolf.
"How wondrous," whispered the moon.

And suddenly Little Wolf knew. He knew why the forest grew. He knew why the earth was wide. He knew why the moon lit up the sky.

The wind ruffled Little Wolf's fur. He listened to the tiny sounds of the forest—a mouse twitching her whiskers, a fawn following her mother.

Then off Little Wolf ran to romp and sing
with his brothers and sisters.

"The forest grows so little mice can play in it," sang Little Wolf. "The earth is wide so elk can leap through the snow."

When Little Wolf stopped to catch his breath, he thought: the wind blows so owls can fly past the stars.

And later that night, as he sat in the light of the moon, he thought: the moon lights up the sky so little wolves can look up at it and wonder.